Allen-Lot.

LILY and the RUNAWAY BABY

By Susan Shreve
Illustrated by Sue Truesdell

A STEPPING STONE BOOK

Random House New York

Text copyright © 1987 by Susan Shreve. Illustrations copyright © 1987 by Sue Truesdell. All rights reserved under International and Pan-American Copyright Conventions. Published in the United States by Random House, Inc., New York, and simultaneously in Canada by Random House of Canada Limited, Toronto.

Library of Congress Cataloging-in-Publication Data:
Shreve, Susan Richards. Lily and the runaway baby. (A Stepping stone book) SUMMARY: Third-grader Lily, a middle child who feels neglected at home, decides to run away and take her infant sister with her. [1. Runaways—Fiction. 2. Brothers and sisters—Fiction] I. Truesdell, Sue, ill. II. Title. PZ7.S55915Li 1987 [E] 87-4684 ISBN: 0-394-89104-X (trade); 0-394-99104-4 (lib. bdg.)

Manufactured in the United States of America   2 3 4 5 6 7 8 9 0

LILY and the
RUNAWAY BABY

ONE

First thing Monday morning, Lily Spencer knew she was going to run away from home the next afternoon, right after her piano lesson. She got out of bed, put on her Disneyland T-shirt and cut-off blue jeans, and went into the bathroom where her sister Melanie was brushing her teeth.

"It's too cold for shorts, Lily," Melanie said. "I heard on the radio."

"Who cares?" Lily replied.

"Who cares?" Jonathan Spencer, Melanie's twin, shot by the bathroom, already dressed for school. "That's all you ever say anymore, Lil-Smil. Who cares? Who cares?" He ran down the steps two at a time.

"So?" Lily shrugged.

"So Mommy thinks you've been in a bad mood lately because of Muffin," Melanie said seriously. Melanie was always trying to teach Lily; she just wasn't very good at it. She was, however, good at everything else—school and sports and making friends. She was only ten and could cook a whole dinner without help. And she had three blue ribbons, two red, four yellow, and one white ribbon for riding.

"Mommy is wrong, of course," Lily said. "I love Muffin."

She brushed her teeth and combed her short, thin, pale-yellow hair.

Then she followed Melanie into her bedroom and flopped across her bed.

"Li-ly," Melanie said. "Please. I just made the bed."

Melanie was very neat. Her books for school were carefully stacked, her shoes were in her shoe bag in the closet, her laundry was in the laundry basket. She didn't even have any toys cluttering her room.

Melanie put daisy barrettes in her neat yellow hair, arranged her stuffed animals on her bed, and went downstairs for breakfast.

"Lily," Mrs. Spencer called. "It's seven thirty."

Lily wandered into Muffin's bedroom and picked her up.

"I'm going to tell you a secret," she said to her baby sister. "You can't tell anyone."

Muffin grabbed a tuft of Lily's chicken-fuzz hair in her tight fist. She cooed happily.

"Tomorrow, after my piano lesson," she whispered to Muffin, "I'm running away from home." She walked down the steps with Muffin in her arms.

In the kitchen Melanie and Jonathan were sitting at the breakfast table, eating granola in silence. Mrs. Spencer was on the telephone with her mother. Happy, the Spencers' Labrador, was eating an English muffin Jonathan had thrown to him under the table.

"Lily," Mrs. Spencer said. "You know I don't like to get Muffin up until I have the rest of you off to school."

"Muffin was crying," Lily said.

"No, she wasn't," Melanie said. "She was very happy."

"She was crying," Lily said. "I'm sorry you're deaf." But she went back upstairs with Muffin just as Mr. Spencer was dashing down.

"Good-bye, Muffin. Good-bye, Lily," he said. "Don't forget to walk Happy this afternoon, Lil."

"Jonathan doesn't do anything ever, of course," Lily said.

But Mr. Spencer was not in the mood to talk about Jonathan this morning.

Lily put Muffin back in her crib.

"So you won't see me again ever," she said to Muffin. "And you don't even care a bit. All you care about is being picked up." And she went downstairs, sat down at the breakfast table, and fixed herself a bowl of granola with eight teaspoons of sugar.

"Sugar makes you hyperactive," Melanie said.

"It would take an electric shock to make Lily hyperactive," Jonathan said.

"Who cares?" Lily said.

"Did you put sugar on the granola?" Mrs. Spencer asked. "There's already natural sugar in it, darling." But she ruffled Lily's hair, and for a split second Lily reconsidered running away from home that afternoon. At least, she thought as she followed Melanie and Jonathan out the front door, her mother might miss her.

TWO

Muffin Spencer, whose real name was Mary Cornelia but who looked, according to Melanie, like a bran muffin, had arrived by surprise. She was not exactly a complete surprise, since Mrs. Spencer, who was forty-two the same day Muffin was born, had been very big for months. But the Spencers had told their older children that the birth of Mary Cornelia had not been in their plans. "A sweet surprise," they called her.

The surprise would have been sweeter, Lily thought, if the Spencers had decided to get a new puppy—perhaps a golden retriever like Anne Claire's. Anne Claire was Lily's best friend.

Once at the dinner table Lily even said that she'd prefer a new puppy to a new baby if she had the choice. But it was perfectly clear, looking at Mrs. Spencer's belly, that there wasn't a choice any longer.

All winter before the baby came Mrs. Spencer paid special attention to Lily.

"The new baby will be hardest on Lily," she told the twins. "She has been the baby for eight years."

"It's not that I'm jealous," Lily said after Muffin was born and had moved into Lily's old room, the one with the window seat. "Muffin is a perfectly okay baby." And she was. She lay on her back smiling happily at nothing all day long. She turned on her stomach and made cooing sounds in her throat. She almost never cried. "It's not that I wonder why you and Daddy decided to get Muffin," Lily said. "What I wonder is why you decided to get me when you already had the twins."

"Lily!" her mother said in a horrified voice. "We wanted you, of course."

On bad days Lily decided she had been adopted.

"How can I be sure I wasn't adopted?" she asked her mother from time to time.

"Believe me," Mrs. Spencer said. "I was there."

"But you are scatterbrained. Even Daddy says so."

"That may be so." Mrs. Spencer laughed. "But I'm certainly not too scatterbrained to remember having you."

Lily was silent. She was not entirely convinced.

"You were the best baby," Mrs. Spencer added. "You played all day by yourself. I hardly knew you were there."

That's exactly how I feel now, especially lately, Lily thought. Lately she was hardly noticed, except when Melanie told her what to do or Mr. Spencer told her not to complain.

In fact, most of the time these days Lily felt miserable. When she looked in the mirror over the dresser in her bedroom, her face was round with baby fat and freckled. She popped the buttons of Melanie's hand-me-down pants because she was too plump. She had gotten three unsatisfactorys on her last report card and a failure in cooperation. "Lily fails to cooperate with me or the class," her homeroom teacher had written in the space for comments. "She has been to the principal's office twice this month." She was no good at sports.

The gym teacher had written that she couldn't do cartwheels or headstands or handstands.

"What *can* you do?" Jonathan had asked her.

"Somersaults. Twenty without stopping,"

Lily had said, and kicked him as hard as she could in the shin.

Even the gym teacher admitted she was good at somersaults. But sometimes somersaults were not enough and she couldn't get to sleep at night for loneliness.

The Spencers were very worried. Mrs. Spencer had already been to Greystone Elementary two times to talk to the teacher about Lily's report card. Mr. and Mrs. Spencer had asked the twins to be very, very considerate of Lily, and Mrs. Spencer made special plans with her as often as she could. But facts were facts; ever since Mary Cornelia Spencer had arrived, Lily had been miserable.

Melanie and Jonathan would whisper secrets back and forth between their rooms. In the big, cozy bedroom at the end of the hall, her parents lay side by side, reading stories to each other. And in Lily's old bedroom, next to her parents' room, Muffin slept softly. If she happened to cry, even for a second, Mrs. Spencer or Mr. Spencer would be up in a flash and take her in bed with them. There she was, Lily Hall Spencer, the only one in the Spencer house who was all by herself.

THREE

The morning of May 1 was warm and sunny, with the sweet smell of honeysuckle in the air. It was perfect weather for running away from home, Lily thought as she followed Melanie and Jonathan into Greystone Elementary.

Anne Claire was standing by the girls' room where she always stood waiting for Lily to arrive at school.

"Guess what?" she said when Lily arrived. Anne Claire always said "Guess what?" as if her life were full of excitement, even though almost nothing ever happened to Anne Claire except the chicken pox in first grade.

"What?" Lily asked.

"Mrs. Jones died!"

"Mrs. Jones? Who is Mrs. Jones?"

"She's the lady who lives across the street from us in the yellow house."

"I never met her."

"Well, now you won't get to," Anne Claire said solemnly. Anne Claire particularly liked bad news. It occurred to Lily that her best friend would be very pleased to hear the bad news that she was running away tomorrow after her piano lesson, but she didn't tell her even when Anne Claire said, "What's your news today?"

"Just the usual news," Lily said. "Did you know Mrs. Jones well?"

"Not so well," Anne Claire said. "I only met her once, when her nurse wheeled her down Maple Avenue to the post office. Would you like to go over and peek in her house with me this afternoon?"

"Creepy," Lily said. "Sometimes you are the creepiest person I know, Anne Claire. Anyway, this afternoon I'm busy."

They walked into homeroom, where to Lily's great surprise and pleasure a substitute teacher sat in the place of Miss Brill. Lily loved the days when Miss Brill was home with her stomach ache, and a substitute who had never heard about Lily's reputation came to class. Those days Lily would be a perfect child. Once in April a substitute had told the principal that Lily Spencer was the best child in the third grade. The principal had called Mrs. Spencer to tell her the good news, and Mrs. Spencer had made a chocolate marshmallow sundae, Lily's favorite dessert, to congratulate her.

In social studies the third grade was studying states. May 1 was the day for New Jersey, which the teacher said was located right next door to New York, where the Spencers lived. Perhaps, Lily thought, she might run away to New Jersey. She could take a train to New York City and then another train to Trenton, New Jersey, which was the capital of New Jersey and which happened to be the only city Lily knew by name.

"How far is it from Scarsdale to Trenton, New Jersey?" Lily asked the substitute teacher during social studies class.

"Three hours by train," the teacher said.

"Why did you need to know?" Anne Claire asked later.

"Because I'm running away to Trenton if things get any worse," Lily said matter-of-factly. She wasn't going to tell Anne Claire that simply no one, including her parents, loved her, but that's the way she felt.

"What would you do in Trenton?" Anne Claire asked as they were sitting on the top bars of the jungle gym. At recess this was where they usually sat to tell secrets.

"Go to an orphanage, I guess," Lily said. "I mean, I'm not exactly old enough to get my own apartment."

"No," Anne Claire agreed. "But you're not an orphan either."

"Well, I am, sort of," Lily said.

That afternoon during library, she asked Mrs. Grenfell, the librarian, to look up orphanages in Trenton, which Mrs. Grenfell did. There was an orphanage called the Trenton Home for Children at 418 Maple Avenue.

The next day, all through math class and language arts and reading and music, Lily made plans. She began writing practice letters to her parents.

Dear Mommy and Daddy and Melanie and Jonathan and Muffin,

I have run away from home as you can see. I am going to the Trenton Home for Children in Trenton, New Jersey, at 418 Maple Avenue. The telephone there is 609-555-1234, if you want to speak to me again. Probably I'll grow up to be famous.

Then she crossed out *famous* and wrote *important*. Then she crossed out *important* and wrote *president*. Then she tore up the whole letter and threw it in the wastebasket and started another letter.

Dear Mommy and Daddy,

I have run away from home and will call you in a few days. The reason why I have run away is because I am VERY UN-HAPPY in this family. I don't belong. You might not even notice that I have left if I didn't write you this note to tell you.

Love,
Lily

She liked that note better. She seemed to have told the exact truth. She drew a picture of a sad girl with a downturned mouth and chicken-fuzz hair. She even wrote the words *chicken fuzz* and made an arrow pointing to the girl's hair. Then she read the letter again and it made her cry. No wonder she said "Who cares?" all the time, she thought to herself. No one cares, no one cares, no one cares. But she wasn't going to tell anyone her plans, not even Anne Claire when they sat on the jungle gym during afternoon recess.

"Do you believe in ghosts?" Anne Claire asked as they sat side by side.

"A little," Lily said. "Once I saw my great-grandmother float into my bedroom and flap around the bookcase, but she was gone by the time I turned on the light."

"Well, I do believe in ghosts," Anne Claire said seriously. "And that's why I want to look into Mrs. Jones's house to see if she is flying around."

"Weird," Lily said thoughtfully.

"I even believe in ghosts when people are alive. Last month when my parents were in Europe, I could feel them in the house. Like they'd left something behind when they went."

"That's only because you remember them so well," Lily said.

"Of course I remember them. They *are* my parents," Anne Claire said. "That's not the point. Their spirits were flapping around the house the whole time they were gone. Even my brother, who is really dumb, noticed."

"Maybe," Lily said. She was not convinced, but she thought about spirits all afternoon during art and study hall and spelling class and detention in the principal's office for talking in math class. If she did have a spirit, she thought, then she would leave part of it behind in the Spencers' house. She liked the idea of her spirit flying through the kitchen while

Mrs. Spencer was cooking, and into Jonathan's model airplane while he was trying to glue it together, and into Melanie's hair while she was doing her homework. But, she thought sadly as she put her books in her book bag when the dismissal bell rang, if they didn't pay attention to Lily Hall Spencer when she was right there in front of them, how were they going to notice an invisible ghost she left behind? They weren't, she thought. And that was that.

She caught up with Jonathan in front of school. Melanie had already gone on the bus to riding, where she was training to be the most famous horseback rider in America. Jonathan had his baseball glove.

"Tell Mom I'm going straight to Little League, okay, Lil?" Jonathan said.

"I'm not supposed to cross Plum Street alone," Lily said.

"Cross with the patrol, then," Jonathan said. "You knew I had to go to Little League."

"What if the patrol is already off duty by the time I get there?"

"Then look both ways and hurry. You're old

enough to cross Plum alone. Melanie and I did it when we were six."

"Who cares?" Lily said. "I could be squished by a car right in the middle of Plum Street and no one would know the difference."

But Jonathan had already gone off to join his friends and did not hear her.

Lily walked home the long way behind the school. By the time she got to Plum Street the patrol boy was off duty, and she had to cross alone for the first time in her life, just as she had suspected. But she had already forgotten to feel sorry for herself, because as she was walking along in the bright sunshine she had a wonderful new idea. It was simply the best idea she had ever had.

This afternoon after piano when she ran away from home, she was not going alone. She would take Mary Cornelia Spencer, called Muffin, with her.

FOUR

Mrs. Spencer was dressed to go out when Lily came home from school.

"Jonathan's at Little League," Lily said. "He'll be home at five."

She didn't tell her mother that Jonathan hadn't bothered to come with her as far as Plum Street so she had had to cross by herself.

The house smelled of fresh-baked cookies, and Lily felt a sudden rush of sadness at leaving her cozy, sweet-smelling home.

"Chocolate chips," Mrs. Spencer said, opening the cookie tin.

Lily took six and poured a glass of milk.

"Why are you so dressed up?" she asked her mother.

Mrs. Spencer put Muffin in her crib.

"I have a meeting at the library, and Mrs.

Treeman is ill and can't take care of Muffin today."

"I'll be glad to watch her." Lily took three more cookies. "Except piano."

"She'll sleep during your piano lesson, I'm sure," Mrs. Spencer said. She kissed the top of Lily's head. "You're a sweetheart. Just call me at the library if there is a problem." She combed her hair and put on lipstick. "Sorry to be in such a rush, Lil. Melanie will be back by five and she can take over."

And Mrs. Spencer was gone.

It was three o'clock by the kitty-cat clock above the sink. At three thirty Mrs. Plaster would come for piano for half an hour. At four thirty Jonathan might be home if practice let out early. So Lily had exactly half an hour to pack her suitcase and Muffin's suitcase, food, and bottles for the trip to Trenton. There was certainly a problem taking Muffin to Trenton, because she had to eat every four hours and she had to be changed every two hours. To be safe Lily had to bring four bottles and eight diapers and a change of clothes. The train to New York left every half-hour, so she could pack her backpack with the clothes and the diapers and the bottles, put Muffin in the portable stroller, leave the house at four, and be at the Scarsdale station in time by walking quickly. In her bank she had $24.68, which she had saved from presents and her allowance. She got the money out, packed her clothes (including Melanie's underpants from Bloomies, which Lily particularly liked), took *Charlotte's Web*, her toothbrush, toothpaste, Pampers, a tiny yellow sweater, and a sweatshirt from her father's college reunion, and went downstairs to fix the bottles. On the counter were six clean bottles, which she filled with milk and put in the top of her book bag.

In the crib Muffin was still sleeping noisily, chewing her tight fist. Lily took a plastic sandwich bag and filled it with chocolate chip cookies. After all, Melanie and Jonathan could have cookies whenever they wished, and she doubted very much that the Trenton Home for Children allowed cookies.

Just as Mrs. Plaster rang the front doorbell Lily finished packing. She had only to write a note to her parents and put Muffin in her portable stroller, and they would be off to Trenton, New Jersey!

Mrs. Plaster was a nervous lady. When Lily said that Muffin just might wake up during the lesson, Mrs. Plaster said she was too nervous to give a proper lesson if there were going to be interruptions. When the telephone call came from Jonathan at Little League to say he wasn't going to be home until six because the team was going to the 7-Eleven to get Slurpees, Mrs. Plaster got up to leave.

"You don't even know your song for today," she whined. "I'm going to speak to your mother again."

Lily was pleased to have Mrs. Plaster leave early, although she pretended to be brokenhearted and promised to work harder than ever next week.

"Seeing is believing," Mrs. Plaster said. She stuffed the music into her bag, picked up her purse, took one chocolate chip cookie, and left.

Lily peered out the living room window and watched Mrs. Plaster until she was down the path and out of sight.

Then she took the folding stroller out of the front closet, got a chewy toy from Muffin's crib, picked Muffin up, and put her in the stroller.

She went upstairs to get her backpack and check herself in the mirror on her closet door. She was not happy with the girl in the mirror. She didn't look old enough to be going on a train to Trenton with a baby. In fact, she looked not a day older than eight years. At the last minute she made a decision to wear blue eyeshadow and bright red lipstick of her mother's. She put the lipstick on carefully and examined herself. She did look older, she decided. Maybe twelve. Then she brushed the chicken fuzz away from her face, rushed downstairs to where Muffin was still sleeping, put her backpack on her shoulders, opened the front door, and left.

All the way to the station she thought about the Trenton Home for Children. She imagined it was a large brick building with ivy, surrounded by a high black gate. The gate was locked. All along the fence children with long faces stood side by side, looking out at the world beyond the orphanage.

"Hello," Lily would say. "I am Lily Hall Spencer and this is Mary Cornelia, my sister."

The children would smile and unlock the gate.

"I have come to live here with you," Lily would say. "My parents didn't want us any longer, especially Muffin. All she does is cry."

The children were thrilled to see Lily. They shouted with excitement and hugged her and grabbed her hand.

"You are just the girl we hoped would come to live with us," they said.

Then Lily imagined that the children took her up the long steps to the orphanage, through the corridor and up the back steps to a small room with a large window overlooking the garden.

"This is the best room," they would say. "We've been saving it for you."

Then she followed them through another corridor to a large room with lots and lots of cribs lined up side by side.

"And this is Muffin's room," they said. "And now we'll go meet the mother in charge of us." They giggled. "She's kind of a witch."

"Don't worry," Lily told the children. "I'm not a bit afraid of witches."

At the corner of Pond Street Lily stopped at the light. She remembered suddenly that she had not written a note to her parents.

Oh, well, she thought. In time the witch at the Trenton Home for Children would call to let them know where Lily and Muffin Spencer were living. And then they would be truly sorry.

FIVE

The clock on top of the Scarsdale railroad station said four twenty-two when Lily crossed Pond Street and pushed Muffin's stroller up to the ticket window to buy a ticket. The station was empty except for a boy about Jonathan's age playing Pac-Man and Miss Velvet, who worked at the candy shop on Main Street.

"Why, hello," Miss Velvet said to Lily. "I'm very pleased to see you." Lily stopped by the candy shop every Saturday after she got her allowance.

"Hello," Lily said. She was not very pleased to see Miss Velvet. She pushed Muffin's stroller straight by Miss Velvet and up to the ticket window. Miss Velvet followed Lily to the ticket window. She leaned over Muffin's stroller and patted her tummy.

"What a sweet baby," she said to Lily. "I

didn't know you had a new baby. I've only seen you and the twins."

Lily asked the ticket man for a ticket to Trenton, New Jersey.

"You can't get a ticket to Trenton, New Jersey, here, honey," the ticket man said. "You have to go to New York and then change to Pennsylvania Station if you want to go to Trenton."

"I see," Lily said.

"You're going to Trenton alone?" Miss Velvet asked.

Lily nodded.

"So do you want a ticket to New York?" the ticket man asked.

"Alone with this baby?" Miss Velvet asked.

Lily nodded.

"Two tickets to New York, then," she said to the ticket man.

"How old are you?"

Lily thought for a moment.

"Ten," she lied.

"It's half-price for you, and the baby's free," the ticket man said.

"Have you just started to wear lipstick?"

Miss Velvet asked. She played with Muffin's feet.

Lily considered. "Since Christmas," she said. "For special occasions."

"What is the special occasion?"

"Going to Trenton," Lily said. She handed the ticket man her money and he gave her a ticket and some change. She now had $21.22 left.

"Is this your first trip alone?" Miss Velvet asked. Now she was playing patty-cake with Muffin.

"No. Muffin and I go to New York all the time," Lily said.

Muffin began to cry. First her face twisted and her fists tightened, and then she let out a terrible scream.

"Oh, dear," Miss Velvet said. "She's crying."

"Yes," Lily said sadly. "But if I push her around the station, she might go back to sleep. See you later."

But Miss Velvet would not be put off. She marched right around the station with Lily, past the wooden benches and the ticket office and the ladies' room and the men's room. All the while Muffin screamed.

"What do you do when she cries like that?" Miss Velvet asked.

"Feed her," Lily said. She was beginning to panic.

"Then feed her."

"On the train," Lily said, rocking the stroller back and forth. "I'll feed her on the train." What if Muffin cried all the way to New York and in the taxicab to Penn Station and on the train to Trenton? Lily might not be allowed to travel with Muffin if she cried like that. The Trenton Home for Children might refuse to take them in.

The ticket man announced the next train over the loudspeaker.

"Time for the train," Miss Velvet said. "You'd better hurry."

Lily pushed Muffin's stroller through the heavy doors onto the platform. The platform was crowded. There were several people on the wooden benches reading the newspaper, and Jimmy Care, whose father owned the Exxon station, was leaning against a post, chewing bubble gum and blowing bubbles. When he heard Muffin's cries, he put his hands over his ears.

"She'll stop soon," Lily said quickly.

"I certainly hope so," a lady next to her said. At just that moment the train to New York rounded the bend at the far end of the tracks and stormed into the station, drowning out the screams of Mary Cornelia Spencer, called Muffin.

SIX

The minute Lily got on the train she noticed a squirrel-cheeked woman in a red dress and a black hat. The woman was staring at Muffin.

"What a cute baby," the woman said, touching Muffin's head. "I love babies. Is she yours?"

Lily nodded.

"A little girl like you, traveling alone?"

Lily didn't answer. Something about the woman made her uneasy. She sat down with Muffin three seats ahead of the squirrel-cheeked woman, but she could still feel the woman's stare through the back of her seat.

Lily tried to feed Muffin, but she refused her bottle. Crying loudly, she spit applesauce on the ankle of a lady with pale-pink nylon stockings who sat in the chair across from Lily.

"These are new stockings," the lady said,

wiping the applesauce off with her hand.

"I'm really sorry," Lily said. She tried again to give Muffin some milk, which she took at first and then threw up on the back of the train seat while Lily burped her.

The lady in pink stockings got up and moved to another part of the train.

Lily tried bouncing Muffin up and down on her lap.

"She'll throw up again," the squirrel-cheeked woman said suddenly. She was standing beside Lily's seat.

"No, she won't," Lily said crossly. But she was wrong. Muffin threw up all over the shoulder of Lily's Greystone Elementary T-shirt.

"I imagine she's also wet," the woman said while Lily cleaned up the mess with her Disneyland T-shirt. The woman reached into Muffin's diapers. "Yes, she is wet," she said.

"I'll change her," Lily said. "Please, Muff." She took out a Pampers. "Please stop crying."

The woman stepped across Lily and sat down.

"Here," she said, and lifted Muffin in her arms. "I'll change her." She put the baby on her lap to change her, and immediately Muffin

stopped crying. She was a grandmother, the woman said to Lily, but her grandchildren were in England and she never saw them. She lived alone in New York City and commuted to work in Scarsdale. She was very lonely, she told Lily. She bounced Muffin on her lap and Muffin cooed happily.

"Where are you going?" the woman asked.

"New York," Lily said. "And then to Trenton."

"Do you travel alone frequently?" the woman asked. "Will someone meet you in New York?"

"My father," Lily said.

"That's nice. And then he'll go with you to Trenton?"

"Maybe," Lily said. The woman in the red dress asked too many questions, but Lily supposed she was pleasant enough. And she had made Muffin stop crying.

The conductor stopped at their seat and took Lily's ticket.

"Why don't you go to the Ladies' and get yourself cleaned up?" the woman said, indicating where Muffin had thrown up on Lily's shirt.

"Next stop in three minutes," called the conductor. "Next stop, Crestwood."

Lily examined her T-shirt. It was still a mess.

"Here," she said, reaching out for Muffin. "I'll take her."

"You just go to the Ladies' and I'll hold your sister until you come back."

Lily hesitated.

"It'll just take you a minute. Your baby will be fine." The woman smiled a broad smile.

Lily reached in her backpack and got her navy blue T-shirt from Larkspur Day Camp, then walked back to the ladies' room.

She had her shirt off when the train stopped. She could hear the conductor call "Crestwood," and she hurried. She did not want to leave Muffin alone with that woman for long. Lily wound her dirty T-shirt in a ball, wiped her shoulder with a wet paper towel, put on the navy blue T-shirt, and checked her face in the mirror for eye shadow and lipstick. The lipstick was smudged and half worn away. She brushed her chicken-fuzz hair with her fingers and then she unlocked the door to the ladies' room. The train was moving again as she went down the aisle to her seat.

The squirrel woman and Muffin were gone.

She ran down the aisle to the place where they had been sitting. They were no longer there. Her backpack was in the seat where she had been sitting, but Muffin's diaper bag had disappeared.

Through the window into the next car, she could see the conductor collecting tickets. She ran down the aisle, through the door.

"My baby sister is gone," she said breathlessly. "That woman in the red dress took her."

The conductor looked confused.

"The woman with the baby?"

Lily nodded.

"She got off the train at Crestwood," he said.

SEVEN

Mrs. Spencer walked in the front door at five thirty to find Jonathan and Melanie sitting side by side on the bottom step of the stairs. She could tell immediately that there was trouble.

"What's the matter?" she asked.

"Lily's gone," Jonathan said.

"She took Muffin," Melanie said. "Miss Velvet who works at the candy store called from the station. She said Lily's on her way to Trenton and did we know."

"Can you believe it?" said Jonathan. "I didn't know Lily had the nerve." He was impressed.

"Did you call Daddy?" Mrs. Spencer asked.

"He's in a meeting."

"Did Miss Velvet say what train she took?"

"I asked," Melanie said proudly. "The four thirty."

Mrs. Spencer checked her watch, picked up the telephone, and called Mr. Spencer in New York. She told Mr. Spencer's secretary there was an emergency and to call him out of the meeting, and she told Mr. Spencer to race to Grand Central Station to meet the four-thirty train from Scarsdale.

"Maybe you can intercept her," Mrs. Spencer said.

Then she looked up Miss Velvet's number in the telephone book. Miss Velvet talked and talked. She told Mrs. Spencer what Lily had been wearing, what Muffin had been wearing, and how sorry she was not to have called the Spencers before the train left.

"I knew she shouldn't be going to New York alone," Miss Velvet said. "But some parents let their children do anything these days."

"Did she say why she was going to Trenton?" Mrs. Spencer asked.

"No. She did say that she goes to New York all the time, though," Miss Velvet said.

"Good heavens!" said Mrs. Spencer. "She's never taken a train trip alone in her entire life!"

Mrs. Spencer called Anne Claire, who said

she had no idea Lily was planning to run away but she had talked a lot that day about Trenton, New Jersey. She had told Anne Claire about the Trenton Home for Children, which was an orphanage; she even had the telephone number.

Finally Mrs. Spencer called the police, who said they would be right over to take a report.

"How do you get to Trenton?" Jonathan asked.

"First you take a train from here to Grand Central Station in New York and then you take a cab to Penn Station and then you take another train to Trenton." Just the thought of her two daughters alone in New York City made Mrs. Spencer ill. "It's very complicated."

Mr. Spencer called from Grand Central Station to say the four-thirty train from Scarsdale was late. Then Mrs. Spencer called the Trenton Home for Children and explained the situation to the director of the home and asked the director to call the Spencers immediately if Lily and Muffin arrived there.

Just as the police knocked on the front door Mr. Spencer called from New York City to say that the four-thirty train from Scarsdale had arrived and Lily was not on it. But Mr. Spencer had spoken to the conductor, who said that Lily had gotten off the train because her baby sister had been stolen by a woman who got off the train with Muffin in Crestwood.

"Stolen?" Mrs. Spencer said.

"I'm going to take the next train to Crestwood."

"Are you sure Muffin was stolen?"

"That's what the conductor said. I'll call you from Crestwood," Mr. Spencer said.

Mrs. Spencer hung up the telephone.

"Stolen?" Melanie asked. "How could Muffin be stolen?"

Mrs. Spencer shook her head and went to the front door. Then she let the policemen in.

EIGHT

Lily got off the train at the stop after Crest-wood. The station was crowded with people arriving from work or waiting to go home. Luckily there was no line at the ticket counter. Lily ran right over.

"I have to go back to Crestwood," she said to the yellow-haired man behind the counter.

"There's a train to Crestwood on the other side of the tracks in about fifteen minutes."

"Fast," Lily said, her heart beating in her throat. "I need to get to Crestwood very fast."

"The train'll be here when it gets here," the man said. "I can't hurry it. Unless you want to take a taxi."

He pointed to the front of the station where three taxicabs were parked with three drivers leaning against their cabs.

Lily ran down the corridor of the station toward the glass doors, and just as she was about to go outside she was stopped by a very small man in a conductor's uniform. "You must be the little girl whose sister was taken off the New York train in Crestwood."

Lily nodded.

"The conductor on your train called and told me you'd be getting off here and for me to help you get a taxi back to Crestwood. I've called the police there, and they'll be meeting you at the station."

"I don't want the police," Lily said, certain she was in enough trouble already. "I can do this myself."

"If someone has stolen your sister, you need the police whether you want them or not."

He helped her into the taxicab.

In the back seat Lily closed her eyes. Her heart was beating fast and hard. Spread across the inside of her eyelids was a soft, sweet image of Muffin. Her eyes were wide-open and terrified; her tiny fists were in her mouth. Muffin. Somehow Lily would have to save her.

The cab stopped at the station, and Lily paid the driver $1.65.

The station was so thick with people that

Lily could see only the long trousered legs and briefcases of businessmen as she peered through the crowd. An announcement on the loudspeaker said the next train to New York was running five minutes late and the north-bound train was arriving on track two. Lily headed toward the ticket counter. There was no chance of finding Muffin in this crowd unless by some good fortune Muffin decided to scream her terrible scream and Lily could hear her above the sound of the train.

A policeman found her just as she hopped up onto a wooden bench, hoping to be tall enough to see the heads of people and not just their legs.

"Are you the little girl with a lost baby?" he asked.

She nodded. "But I can find her myself," she said. "That's what I'm doing now."

The policeman lifted her down from the bench.

"I'm here to help you," he said. "Now sit and tell me exactly what happened."

Lily did not have a choice. He sat her down beside him and listened carefully as she described the woman who had stolen Muffin from the train.

"What were you doing alone on a train to New York, anyway?" the policeman asked Lily.

"Running away," she told him matter-of-factly. She did not tell him she had taken Muffin because she thought her family preferred Muffin to her. In fact, she no longer even believed that. She thought of her mother with a sudden sadness. In Lily's mind Mrs. Spencer was sitting in the kitchen with her hands folded tightly together, very worried. "Perhaps you could call my mother for me," she said to the policeman, but he had gotten up to speak with another policeman and then another and then another. The station was full of policemen.

"Stay here," the first policeman said to Lily. "We're going to check the crowd to see if anyone has seen the kidnapper and your baby sister."

For a moment Lily sat exactly as she had been told to do. The clock above the ticket window said five thirty. The squirrel-cheeked woman had arrived with Muffin almost half an hour ago. Certainly they wouldn't still be in the station. Maybe they had taken a taxi to another town or another state, like New Jersey. It occurred to Lily that Muffin could be lost for good. She might never see her again. And Lily's heart ached. She could not wait for the policemen to find Muffin. She leaped up, rushed across the station to the front door, past two policemen questioning a woman in a business suit with a briefcase, through the door, and out onto the main street of Crestwood. She would find Muffin herself.

Across the street from the station were rows of shops, and Lily went first to Harvey's Dry Cleaning.

"No," the round lady at the counter said after Lily had described Muffin and the woman to her. "I'm sorry to say I haven't seen either of them."

"No," the young boy at Ring's Ice Cream said. "Nobody's been in with a baby since I came to work at noon."

"No," the young girl at the bookstore said. "There was a grandmother here a little while ago with her granddaughter but no one with a baby since this morning."

Lily crossed the street and went into the drugstore, where a very small woman with bright red hair peered over the counter.

"A baby with an older woman?" she repeated after Lily.

"The baby's about this big." Lily held out her arms to Muffin's size. "She's wearing a yellow sweater."

"There was a woman here with a baby just a few minutes ago." The small red-haired woman shook her head. "The baby was screaming at the top of her lungs. So the woman bought a pacifier and a package of peanut M & M's. She unwrapped the pacifier right away and put it in the baby's mouth, but it didn't work."

"Where did they go?"

"They just left." She pointed in the direction away from the railroad station. "If you hurry, you'll catch them."

Lily ran straight down Main Street, past the flower shop, the co-op grocery store, and the Crestwood post office, past the bus stop and the unisex hair salon to the traffic light at Main, which was red. When she stopped, she heard the faroff cry of a baby.

Her heart was beating so fast it felt as if it would jump out of her chest. She could not breathe. But she listened. Above the sounds of cars, she distinctly heard the sound of a baby. The light turned green and then red again, but still she listened, hoping to trace the sound and follow it.

And she did. She raced down the block past a woman in purple trousers walking a Labrador retriever, past four boys in soccer uniforms, and past two elderly women arm in arm. The baby's cry was louder. Just as she came to the end of the block, she saw the squirrel-cheeked woman. Muffin's tiny head was bobbing on the woman's shoulder.

"Muffin!" Lily cried, racing down the block.

"Muffin!" she shouted. She could run much faster than the woman. "Wait," Lily said. And in seconds, dizzy with excitement, she had caught up to them.

Without a word the squirrel-cheeked kidnapper handed Muffin to Lily and rushed down the street, not terribly fast because she was not young.

"Oh, Muffin," Lily said, hugging her tight. Muffin smiled a sunny smile and buried her

face in Lily's shoulder. "I'm so happy to see you."

There was a laundry on the corner, and Lily went in and asked the young boy who worked there to call the police for her, which he did.

"My baby sister was stolen on the train to New York and I just found her," she told the boy.

"Amazing." He dialed the police. "Who stole her?"

"Just some woman."

He handed Lily the phone. "I am Lily Spencer," she said. "The girl whose baby was stolen. I have found her." She told the police she was at the laundry and the kidnapper was very close-by.

"We'll be right there," the policeman said.

And they were.

The patrol car drove up to the laundry and the policeman from the railroad station hopped out.

"So you found her," he said, tousling Lily's hair. "All by yourself."

"I lost her by myself too," Lily said.

"Well, your father's at the railroad station. He's going to be very glad to see you," he said, and opened the door of the patrol car for Lily to get in.

"And we have caught the woman who stole your baby sister," the policeman said, getting in beside Lily. "She is not an ordinary criminal."

"What kind of criminal is she?" Lily asked.

"Just a lonely woman who decided she wanted a baby," he said.

Lily settled into the front seat. Muffin had stopped crying. She settled comfortably in Lily's lap and munched her new pacifier. Lily patted her silken cheek.

"I'm so glad to see you, Muffin," she whispered.

In a matter of minutes she would see her father at the Crestwood train station. He would be in his navy blue business suit with a briefcase and a newspaper under his arm. He was going to be very angry.

He would be right, too. Lily had taken a great risk with her life and with Muffin's. She had frightened her mother and father and even the twins. At this very moment Muffin could have been in grave danger. Lily's arms tightened around her sister. She knew she had been very lucky.

First thing after she got home and promised her mother and Melanie and Jonathan that she'd never do such a thing again, she was going to call Anne Claire.

"Guess what?" she'd say to Anne Claire. And then she'd tell her the whole story.

"I suppose that's the worst true story I have ever heard," Anne Claire would say solemnly.

"So if I were you, I wouldn't run away from home ever."

"I won't," Anne Claire would say. "I like it very much at home, even though my brother lives here."

"Me too," Lily would reply. "I think I even love the twins."

The police car pulled up to the Crestwood station. In the distance Lily saw her father walking toward her, and her heart beat double time.

She sat Muffin up on her lap.

"So, Muffin," she said softly. "We had a terrible adventure and we'll never run away from

home again." And she kissed her sister's tiny
fingers one by one.

ABOUT THE AUTHOR

SUSAN SHREVE is a well-known author of books for children, including the recent *The Flunking of Joshua T. Bates*. She based *Lily and the Runaway Baby* on a true story from her own childhood. "When I was six years old, I had an argument with my parents and left home with my baby brother," she says. "I was afraid that if I ran away alone my parents would be very relieved. But if I took my baby brother Jeff, then they'd be sorry." Both children were returned home by the local police in Washington, D.C., where Susan Shreve still lives with her four children and her husband.

ABOUT THE ILLUSTRATOR

SUE TRUESDELL always wanted to be a children's book illustrator. The books she has illustrated for young readers include *Addie Meets Max*, *Dabble Duck*, and *The Pirate Who Tried to Capture the Moon*.